D0358612

SHEILA RAE, THE BRAVE

Kevin Henkes
VIKING KESTREL

VIKING KESTREL

Published by the Penguin Group
27 Wrights Lane, London W8 5TZ, England
Viking Penguin Inc., 40 West 23rd Street, New York, New York 10010, USA
Penguin Books Australia Ltd, Ringwood, Victoria, Australia
Penguin Books Canada Ltd, 2801 John Street, Markham, Ontario, Canada L3R 1B4
Penguin Books (NZ) Ltd, 182–190 Wairau Road, Auckland 10, New Zealand

Penguin Books Ltd, Registered Offices: Harmondsworth, Middlesex, England

First published in the USA by Greenwillow Books 1987
First published in Great Britain by Viking Kestrel 1988

Copyright © 1987 by Kevin Henkes

All rights reserved. Without limiting the rights under copyright
reserved above, no part of this publication may be reproduced,
stored in or introduced into a retrieval system, or transmitted, in any form
or by any means (electronic, mechanical, photocopying, recording or
otherwise), without the prior written permission of both the copyright
owner and the above publisher of this book.

British Library Cataloguing in Publication Data

Henkes, Kevin
Sheila Rae, the brave.
I. Title
823'.914 [J]   PZ7

ISBN 0-670-82157-8

Printed in Hong Kong by
Imago Publishing Ltd

For Gretchen

Sheila Rae wasn't afraid of anything.

She wasn't afraid of the dark.

She wasn't afraid of thunder and lightning.

And she wasn't afraid of the big black dog
at the end of the road.

At dinner, Sheila Rae made believe that the cherries
in her fruit salad were the eyes of dead bears,
and she ate five of them.

At school, Sheila Rae giggled when the headteacher walked by.

And when her classmate, Wendell, stole her skipping rope
during break, Sheila Rae tied him up until the bell rang.
"I am very brave," Sheila Rae said, patting herself on
the back.

Sheila Rae stepped on every crack in the pavement without fear.

When her sister, Louise, said there was a monster in the cupboard, Sheila Rae attacked it.

And she rode her bicycle no-handed with her eyes closed.
"Yea! Yea! Sheila Rae!" her friends yelled,
clapping their hands.

One day, Sheila Rae decided to walk home from
school a new way. Louise was afraid to.
"You're too brave for me," Louise said.

"You're always such a scaredy-cat," Sheila Rae called.
"Am not," whispered Louise.

Sheila Rae started off, skipping.
"I am brave," she sang. "I am fearless."

She stepped on every crack.

She walked backwards with her eyes closed.

She growled at stray dogs,

and bared her teeth at stray cats.

And she pretended that the trees were evil creatures.
She climbed up them and broke their fingers off.
Snap, snap, snap.

Sheila Rae walked and walked.

She turned corners.

She crossed roads.

It suddenly occurred to Sheila Rae that
nothing looked familiar.

Sheila Rae heard frightening noises.
They sounded worse than thunder.

She thought horrible thoughts.
They were worse than anything she had ever imagined.
"I am brave," Sheila Rae tried to convince herself.
"I am fearless."

The sounds became more frightening.
The thoughts became more horrible.
Sheila Rae sat down on a rock and cried.
"Help," she sniffed.

She thought of her mother and her father and Louise.
"Mother! Father! Louise!" she cried.

"Here I am," a voice said.

"Louise!" Sheila Rae hugged her sister.
"We're lost," Sheila Rae said.
"No, we're not," said Louise. "I know the
way home. Follow me!"

Louise stepped on every crack.

She walked backwards with her eyes closed.

She growled at stray dogs, and bared
her teeth at stray cats.

And she pretended that the trees were evil creatures.
She jumped and broke their fingers off.
Snap, snap, snap.
Sheila Rae walked quietly behind her.

They walked and walked.

They crossed roads.

They turned corners.

Soon their house could be seen between the trees.
Sheila Rae grabbed Louise and dashed up the street.

When they reached their own garden and the gate was closed behind them, Sheila Rae said, "Louise, you are brave. You are fearless."

"We both are," said Louise.
And they walked backwards into the house
with their eyes closed.